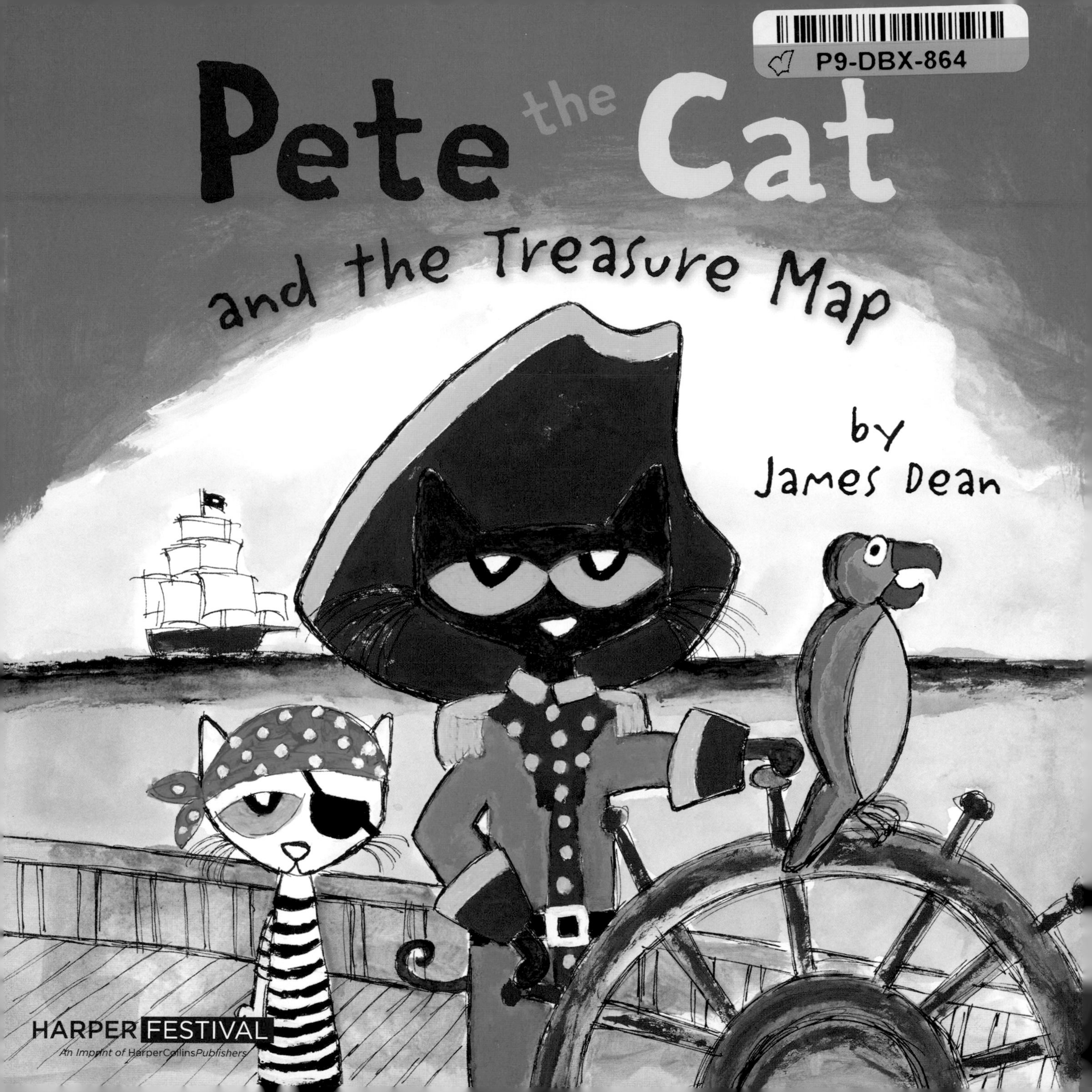
Pete the Cat
and the Treasure Map
by
James Dean
HARPER FESTIVAL
An Imprint of HarperCollinsPublishers

HarperFestival is an imprint of HarperCollins Publishers.

Pete the Cat and the Treasure Map

www.harpercollinschildrens.com

Library of Congress Control Number: 2016938983
ISBN 978-0-06-269914-5

The artist used pen and ink, with watercolor and acrylic paint, on 300lb hot press paper to create the illustrations for this book.

18 19 20 21 SCP 10 9 8 7 6 5

❖

First Edition

Captain Pete looks across Cat Cove. The sun is sparkling on the water. It's a beautiful day for an adventure!

Something flies toward Captain Pete's ship. It's a parrot!

"Squawk!" says the parrot. She gives Captain Pete a crumpled piece of paper.

"What is it?" asks First Mate Callie.

Captain Pete looks at the paper. There's a long trail that ends with an X. "It's a treasure map!" he says.

"Treasure!" says First Mate Callie. "Where?"

"On Secret Island," says Captain Pete.

"Let's go!" says First Mate Callie.

"Woo-hoo!" cries the crew. "Treasure!"

Captain Pete steers the ship through the big waves. The salty wind pushes the sails. The ship is going really fast.

"Good job, mateys," says Captain Pete.
"We'll be there in no time!"

Uh-oh. Captain Pete spoke too soon.
He spies something coming toward them.
"What is that?" asks First Mate Callie.

A giant arm reaches up and splashes the water. It makes a wave that crashes down on Pete's boat.

"Squawk," cries the parrot.

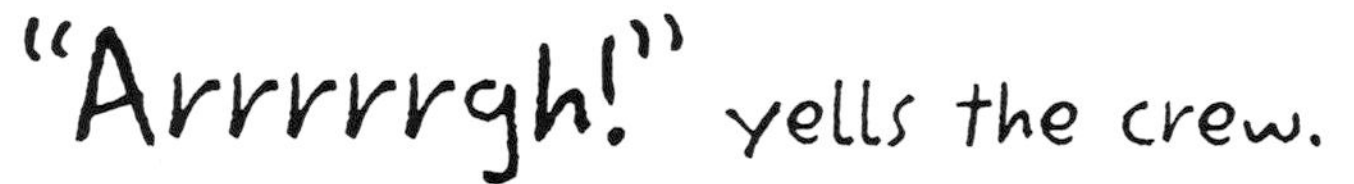

"Arrrrrgh!" yells the crew.

KRR-SPLASH! Another arm comes crashing down.

The crew is scared, but not Captain Pete.
He knows that the monster isn't trying to scare them. He's rocking a cool beat.

Captain Pete takes out his guitar and strums. The monster rises out of the water. The crew takes cover, but the monster stops when he hears Pete playing.

He nods his head along. He's not a scary sea monster—
he's an awesome sea drummer!

"Rock on!" says Captain Pete.
"Thanks!" booms the monster.

"Oh no, captain!" shouts First Mate Callie. "A big storm is coming!"

"Batten down the hatches!" says Captain Pete. Everyone gets ready for the storm.

The waves toss the ship, but the crew is brave.

Captain Pete has an idea. "Hey there, friend!" he yells to the sea monster. "We need some help."

The monster grabs the ship with his giant arms and gives it a great big boost.

The ship moves right through the storm!

"Hooray!" shouts the crew as the monster swims up to the boat.

"Thanks, friend!" yells Captain Pete.
"No problem," booms the monster.

"Land ho!" yells First Mate Callie, pointing out over the sea. All the pirates rush to look.

"It's Secret Island!" says Captain Pete.

On the beach, their buddy Grumpy Toad is waiting with a glittering pile of treasure!

"Ahoy, mateys. You got my map!" Grumpy Toad says. "Treasure is no fun if you can't share it with your friends."

The crew is so happy, they do cat-wheels in the sand. "Thanks, Grumpy Toad!" they shout.

"I think we're missing something," says Captain Pete. "Let's play some music!"

"What a great idea!" says Grumpy Toad.

The pirates load all the treasure onto the ship. Captain Pete takes out his guitar and strums. But something is missing from his song. . . .

"Our drummer," Captain Pete says as the sea monster pops his head above the waves. "Would you like to join my crew?"

"AYE!" booms the monster.

"Rock on!" Captain Pete says as the monster joins in on a rockin' pirate tune.

Captain Pete's crew is complete. All the pirates sing,

"Yo ho, yo ho, a pirate's life for us!"